THE
WICKFORD
DOOM

THE WICKFORD DOOM

CHRIS PRIESTLEY

With illustrations by
VLADIMIR STANKOVIC

Barrington Stoke

First published in 2015 in Great Britain by
Barrington Stoke Ltd
18 Walker Street, Edinburgh, EH3 7LP

www.barringtonstoke.co.uk

Text © 2015 Chris Priestley
Illustrations © 2015 Vladimir Stankovic

A CIP catalogue record for this book is available
from the British Library upon request

ISBN: 978-1-78112-409-3

Printed in China by Leo

For Anne & Tim

The air-raid siren sounded just as Harry and his mother sat down to dinner. They would just have to eat the food cold when they got back from the shelter. It wouldn't be the first time – or the last.

They had an Anderson shelter in the back garden. Harry had helped his father to build it. It was only a few yards from the back door but they walked as fast as they could, heads down, hand in hand. Harry's mother seemed to hold her breath until they arrived.

They sat silent, as always. Harry's mother held his hand so hard it hurt – but Harry never complained. They listened to the muffled thud of bombs and guns and comforted themselves with the thought that they sounded far off tonight.

Then the all-clear sounded and they could go back inside. Harry saw their neighbours doing the same, but no one spoke. The family had moved here just before Harry's father got his call-up to the army and they had never got to know anyone very well.

At first, when Harry's father was away, it felt as if Harry's mum was waiting for him to come home all the time. Waiting for him to come back so they could live proper lives again.

When they learned that he would never come home, Harry knew she felt it was wrong to live at all. She felt like it was wrong to live like normal people – like they were pretending that their lives had not been ruined for ever by the letter that came to say his father had been killed in action.

That night, Harry woke in the small hours. It was so dark that there seemed little difference between his eyes being open or shut, but at last he began to make things out in the gloom. He heard something, too.

It was the sound of sobbing. Harry crept out of bed and along the hall. A lamp was on in the sitting room.

Harry stood at the door and saw his mother sitting in the armchair. Her head was bent, and she had a hanky in one hand and a photograph in a frame in the other.

Harry could only see the back of the photograph but he knew what it was. It was a photo of his father in uniform in the desert, a smile on his face.

Harry's mother looked up and saw him standing there.

"Oh, Harry," she said. "I'm sorry ..."

Harry walked into the room and they hugged and his mother cried some more. Harry cried too, for all that he tried not to, because his father had told him to be brave and look after his mother when he wasn't there.

But it was hard.

The next day was Saturday and after breakfast
Alan and Eric knocked at the door to see if
Harry wanted to play football.

Harry was not close friends with Alan or
Eric, but sometimes he needed to get out. Time
seemed to have come to a stop inside the house
and it felt so good to play and not think, to run
free like an animal.

The boys kicked the ball around in the
street until a group of younger children
turned up and there were enough of them to

play something like a proper game. Harry's team lost 5–3 after the usual fierce flash of arguments about handballs and fouls and goals or no goals.

Then the young ones ran off to play hide and seek in a bomb site while Harry, Alan and Eric sat on the kerb to get their breath back.

They chatted about the air raid the night before and Alan said that it had been pretty bad. His father was an ARP warden, and he'd told Alan that the wall of a burning warehouse had collapsed on two firemen, and killed them both.

Harry's heart was always heavy after football. While the game lasted, it was like an oasis in the dull, bomb-cratered desert they lived in now. A place where he could forget the world, forget the war. But bit by bit, it always seeped back in.

When he walked in the door at home, Harry found his mother sitting at the table with a stern-looking man in a dark suit.

"Harry," his mother said. "This is Mr Williams."

Mr Williams got to his feet and held out his hand for Harry to shake. "Pleased to meet you, Harry," he said.

"Hello, sir."

"Mr Williams is a lawyer," Harry's mother said. "He has some exciting news."

Harry had no real idea what a lawyer did apart from stand up in court with a wig on. But he had the distinct feeling that whatever this man did, it wasn't fun. He didn't look like someone who was about to tell them anything exciting.

"Harry," Mr Williams said. "I am the lawyer for your father's family in Suffolk."

"But Dad hated his family," Harry said.

"Harry!" his mother cried.

Mr Williams's thin face cracked into a half-smile.

"That may be," he said, "but despite that, your father's cousin remembered your father in his will."

Harry's eyes grew wide. "They were rich, weren't they?" he said.

"They were," Mr Williams said. "Very rich at one time and still rather well-off."

"Are we going to be rich?" Harry asked. "Are we rich, Mum?"

"Shhh," his mother said. "Let Mr Williams speak."

"Your father's cousin left your father a piece of property in Suffolk," the lawyer went on. "A house and some land at a place called Wickford. Part of what had been a rather large estate."

"Goodness!" Harry's mother said. "Wickford Hall?"

She and Harry looked up at a small dark painting above the fire. It showed a gloomy manor house – a house Harry's father had always said they should live in, if only they hadn't been cheated out of it by some relative or other.

"Imagine, Harry!" Harry's mother said, and she pointed to the painting.

Harry saw the lawyer open his mouth as if he was going to say something, but then he changed his mind and smiled a forced smile instead.

"I'm afraid I am not free at the moment to give any more details about the will," Mr Williams said. "My orders were to ask you to travel to Suffolk where ... well, I will explain then."

Harry's mother turned to him, beaming. "Suffolk, Harry?" she said. "How do you like the sound of that? Get away from these bombs for a while."

"We will, of course, be happy to pay your expenses," the lawyer said.

"Gosh," Harry's mother said. "A free trip to the seaside, Harry. Or ..."

She turned to the lawyer.

"Wickford Hall is on the coast, isn't it?" she asked.

"Oh yes," he said. "Very much so."

Again the lawyer looked as if he was going to say more, but instead he folded his fingers together and said that he had to be going.

"I'm going to Suffolk myself this afternoon," he said. "I have taken the liberty of arranging train tickets for you and your son for tomorrow, if that suits."

"I dare say we'll manage to make the journey, won't we, Harry?" Harry's mother said. "You might have to miss a couple of days at school."

Mr Williams shook Harry's mother by the hand and nodded to Harry. He put on his hat, picked up his briefcase and umbrella, then took his leave.

Harry peered out of the window as Mr Williams walked off up the street. When he got to the corner he turned and looked back at their house for a moment. Then he shook his head and walked on.

Harry had a strong feeling that there was more to this business than the lawyer was letting on, but he didn't have the heart to say anything to his mother. Besides, it was only a hunch – what would he have said?

But the niggling doubt wouldn't go away. It seemed like such good news. What could possibly be wrong? Maybe Harry had just forgotten how to enjoy life.

For the 100th time, Harry wished his father was there. He wished he could talk to him and ask him what he thought. In fact, he just wished that his father could take care of everything and leave Harry to be a boy again.

Harry felt sure his father would have had doubts about the lawyer too. But he wasn't there. He was never coming back and that was that.

It had been a long time since Harry had been
on a train and his worries began to fade as
he looked out of the window at the rolling
countryside. It all looked so normal here, away
from the city. It was almost possible to pretend
the war was over.

There were trees and fields and church
spires, just as they had always been. There was
a farmer in his tractor, followed by gulls as he
dug up the earth. Harry knew that the war had
infected every part of the country, but here it
didn't look so sick, so broken.

Mr Williams, the lawyer, was there to meet them at the station at Talmington. He had on the same dark suit and stiff white collar and tie.

He smiled in his cold way and asked them about their journey, and again Harry had the sudden feeling that something was not quite right. Harry's doubts must have shown on his face, because the lawyer frowned and his manner changed.

"I think I should say that I have acted as your father's cousin's will said I must," he said. The platform had cleared and the train had moved on.

Harry thought Mr Williams sounded a bit defensive. As if they had accused him of something. Or they would do.

"I'm sure you have –" Harry's mother began.

"I'm sorry to interrupt you, Mrs Pointer," Mr Williams said, "but I must explain. I followed the will to the letter. That is my duty as a lawyer. I hope you will forgive me."

"Forgive you?" Harry's mother said. "What is there to forgive?"

The lawyer's smile had now vanished.

"The last step laid out in the will," he said, "is that I must take you to view the property. Without any further explanation."

"I see," Harry's mother said. "This is all very mysterious."

"I have a car," Mr Williams said. "If you'd like to follow me, I'll take you there now. It's only a short drive."

It was only the second time in Harry's life that he had ever ridden in a car – and never in such a nice one – but he did his best to look as if he did it every day. He looked out of the window and marvelled at the amount of sky he could see and the trees and flowers everywhere. It was so different to London that it might just as well have been the Amazon jungle or the Sahara desert.

After about five minutes they headed down a narrow lane that took them between fields with tall hedges and leafy trees on either side. Then they turned again at a metal signpost that said 'Arlham 1 mile'.

As they came over a hill, Harry got his first glimpse of the sea in the distance and he couldn't stop himself giving a little cry of excitement. His mother grinned.

"The sea!" she said. "How lovely."

In truth, it did not look very lovely today. The sky was grey and the sea even more so. Harry looked in the rear-view mirror and saw the lawyer's eyes looking back at him. As soon as their eyes met, Mr Williams looked back to the road. They headed downhill until they reached a village with an old church and a cluster of buildings around a green and a pond.

"This is Arlham," Mr Williams said, as they drove through the village and out onto a road that ran between bare thorn hedges. Now they were heading for the coast.

After a while they turned at a stone gate and drove up a long gravel track. Harry's mother turned and looked at him, her eyes shining. Harry pressed his face against the glass, trying to see what was ahead.

They came to a stop near a little cottage and when they got out of the car they saw that the track ahead came to a sudden end.

There was a barrier in front of the car that looked like it had been put there by the army. But beyond that, Harry could see that the track fell off the edge of the cliff as if it was the end of the world.

"I don't understand," Mrs Pointer said, as Harry walked to the end of the track and looked past the barrier and over the cliff to the beach below.

"Not too close, young man," Mr Williams called. "The cliffs are very unstable."

"Come away, Harry!" his mother said. "Where are we?" she asked the lawyer. "I thought you were taking us to Wickford Hall."

Mr Williams stared at his shoes for a moment and took a deep breath.

"This is ... very ... difficult," he said. "Wickford Hall fell over that cliff 40 years ago. Every stone of it is under the sea."

Harry and his mother stared off at the cliff and then back at Mr Williams. The lawyer licked his lips as though his mouth had gone dry.

"What on earth do you mean?" Harry's mother said.

"I'm afraid that this was a rather nasty joke meant for your husband," the lawyer said. "I was bound by the will to bring him here without any explanation. And since your husband has passed away, I'm afraid –"

"My husband did not 'pass away', as you put it," Harry's mother said. "My husband was killed in the service of this country. He was a good man. Too good for this cruel game. You should be ashamed of yourself."

"And I am," Mr Williams said with a sigh. "But I am a lawyer and I must obey my client's wishes, however unpleasant."

Harry's mother shook her head, unable to speak. Harry scowled. Then the sound of tyres on the track made them all turn to see a black car arrive. It parked on the grass and the driver got out and walked towards them.

"Ah," Mr Williams said. "Mr Slater. Mr Slater, this is Mrs Pointer and her son, Harry."

Mr Slater offered his hand. Harry's mother hesitated for a moment, but in the end she shook it. Harry went on scowling.

Mr Slater was a round and red-faced man who looked like he had stepped out of a photograph from the 1850s. He was wearing a tweed suit with a gold watch chain and he had a huge moustache that curled over his mouth and hid it from sight.

"Mr Slater has been looking after the estate for some years," Mr Williams said.

"You must be a good swimmer then, Mr Slater," Harry's mother said.

"Ah," Mr Slater said, and he looked puzzled for a moment. "Well ... yes. Quite. But not all the estate is under the waves. There is a little land. Did Mr Williams tell you about the cottage?"

"I was just about to," Mr Williams said. "But, Mrs Pointer, perhaps it is best that I leave you in the care of Mr Slater. I have booked you into the inn in Arlham village. I will, of course, cover the bill."

"Thank you," Harry's mother said. "That will not be necessary."

Mr Williams bowed and tipped his hat.

"The room is there," he said. "You will need a place to stay tonight. The next train doesn't leave until the morning."

He handed Harry's mother a large envelope.

"This contains all the papers about the estate. If you have any questions at all, please do contact me."

He handed her a card, but she did not take it. He tried to give it to Harry instead, but Harry looked away.

"As you wish," Mr Williams said, with another bow. "Good day, Mrs Pointer. Master Pointer. Mr Slater, if you could call me later. I will be staying at the Rose and Crown until tomorrow."

With that, he tipped his hat again and walked to his car. A minute later he was just a cloud of dust in the distance. Harry kicked a stone and it bounced into a ditch. He strode off across the meadow and pretended not to hear his mother when she called him back.

Harry was angry. He was angry with Mr Williams for tricking them, angry with his mother for being tricked, but angry most of all with himself for not having the guts to say he was worried right from the start.

He stopped and looked back. His mother and Mr Slater were deep in conversation. Harry sighed and walked a little further until he came to the wall at the cliff's edge.

He picked up a stick and walked along, swishing it at the weeds as he passed. As he walked past the door in the wall, he thought he heard something and stopped.

The sea was pounding on the beach below the cliffs, the wind was rustling the tree branches high above, and sea birds wept and cried all around. But there was something else.

Harry tried to focus in on this other noise and realised it seemed to be coming from behind the door. It sounded like whispering.

Harry put one hand on the rusty old padlock and the other on the looped handle of the door. Then he leaned forward and pressed his face and ear to the peeling paint. All of a sudden the door swung open and Harry found himself staring down at the beach a hundred feet below him.

Harry yelled out in panic and tried to pull himself back, but the door seemed to have a life of its own. It tugged against him, dragging him towards the cliff. The toes of his shoes slid towards the edge. He knew that at any second he would be dangling from the door handle alone.

Then there were arms around him and Mr Slater was pulling him back from the edge. Harry's mother ran to meet them as Mr Slater dragged Harry across the grass.

"My God, Harry!" she said. "What were you thinking?"

"It was locked, Mum!" he said. "I swear it was."

"It can't have been," she said in horror. "You could have been killed. He could have been killed!"

Mr Slater pulled the door shut and snapped the padlock back in place.

"I've never seen that door unlocked," he said. "Never."

"Another joke perhaps?" Mrs Pointer said. Her face was pale with shock and anger.

"A joke?" Mr Slater said. "Come now. What do you take us for? Why would I – or anyone else – wish the boy harm? We've had some tragedies ourselves in the past and –"

"I'm sorry," Harry's mother broke in. "You saved Harry's life just now. I should thank you."

Harry recovered his wits for the first time since he had hung over the void. "Yes, thank you," he said.

"You're welcome, young man," said Mr Slater.

Harry stared back at the door and at the death he had cheated. He looked at the rusty old padlock. It looked as though it hadn't been touched for years. Just as it had when he put his hand on it to listen for whispers at the door.

There was a strained silence as they walked
back to Mr Slater's car after the near disaster
at the cliff. Mr Slater rubbed his hands
together and smiled, but he still looked nervous.
Harry's mother stared off towards the sea and
Harry saw the glint of a tear on her cheek.

"You must be very tired," Mr Slater said at
last. "After your journey and so forth."

"Yes," Harry's mother said. She didn't look
at him.

"Would you like to see the cottage?" he asked, with a forced smile. "As we're here. It's a pretty little place."

"I suppose we should," Harry's mother said. Her voice was flat and cold. "After all, we have come all this way. Then you and Mr Williams can have a jolly good laugh at us when we're gone."

Mr Slater frowned.

"Laugh?" he said. "No, no. You have quite the wrong idea. I have never met Mr Williams before in my life. We have written letters about the estate, but that's all. I had imagined he would have made everything clear to you before he brought you here. You mustn't think that I ..."

Harry's mother sighed and reached out to hold Harry's hand.

"I'm very sorry," she said. "I am a little upset."

"Of course you are," Mr Slater said. "Who wouldn't be? It's a nasty trick and, well … I won't speak ill of the dead, but it's just the sort of thing I would have expected of his lordship. Forgive my bluntness, but we won't miss him much."

Mr Slater started to walk back towards his car and Harry and his mother followed behind.

"We never saw much of him," Mr Slater said. "The family bought a new house inland when Wickford Hall went into the sea. He spent most of his time in London, in any case."

The cottage was sat back a little from the road. It had pink walls, small windows and a tiled roof. Harry thought it looked like the kind of house that appeared in fairy tales. But this was no fairy tale, it seemed. Or not one with a happy ending.

Mr Slater led the way. He took a large key from his pocket, opened the door and let them in. The door was low and led into the living room. There was a brick fireplace at one end and a door on one side into the kitchen.

"I've lit a fire in your rooms," Mr Slater said. "It can get a bit chilly at nights. The cottage just needs to be lived in for a bit."

"That's very kind of you," Harry's mother said. "But we shan't be staying."

"Oh?" Mr Slater said. "I just thought … Since you've come all this way and the cottage is yours –"

"Even so," Harry's mother said. "Thank you."

"As you wish," Mr Slater said. "I'll drive you to the village."

Harry's mother turned to leave, but all of a sudden Harry was desperate to see the rest of the cottage. It was theirs, after all. They couldn't just walk away before they had seen it.

"Mum?" Harry said, and he reached out to take her arm. "Can't we just have a look?"

His mother gave a weak smile. She thought for a moment and then sighed.

"Of course we can, Harry," she said. "If you want to."

"Thanks, Mum," Harry said. "Can we go upstairs first?"

Mr Slater led the way up the stairs. They were steep and narrow, almost like a ladder. At the top, he opened the door in front of him.

"We put this bathroom in a couple of years back," he said. "It's better kitted out than my own house."

There were two bedrooms, one above the living room, the other above the kitchen. One had a double bed, the other a single. Both had timber beams in the sloping ceiling.

"Wow!" Harry said. "Look, Mum. Look how old it is."

"It was built when the old Hall was built, we reckon," Mr Slater said. "That makes it about 500 years old."

Harry whistled, his eyes wide. "Gosh," he said.

His mother chuckled. "Harry loves history," she said.

"There was a whole village here then," Mr Slater said. "It's all gone now. There's only this house, the church tower and the old wall over there."

He pointed out of the window at a high wall running in line with the cliff edge along a meadow beside the road – the wall with the door Harry had almost fallen through.

"It used to be the wall at the end of the garden," Mr Slater said. "A lovely garden too. All gone. All gone."

Mr Slater showed them round the rest of the house. In the kitchen, a lantern lit the room with a warm glow and there was heat from the cooking range. On the table were some eggs, a loaf and a small pie.

"The missus made the pie for you," Mr Slater said.

"She shouldn't have," Harry's mother said. "And eggs!"

"We have our own chickens," Mr Slater said. "We know how hard it is in London. It's a bit easier here. We've had electricity put into the cottage too," he added. "But it's a little temperamental. There's a storm forecast, so I've left you plenty of candles and lamps –"

"We're not staying, Mr Slater," Harry's mother said. "But thank you for being so kind."

"Oh, Mum!" Harry said. "Please can we stay?"

His mother sighed and put her arm around him.

"Please, Mum," he said. "Why not? We own it. And we'll only bump into that Mr Williams if we stay in the inn."

"All right," she said after a moment. "As Mrs Slater has gone to all this trouble."

"It wasn't any trouble," Mr Slater said with a smile. "She was happy to do it."

He showed them all the rooms in the house
again, and explained where everything they
would need was, and how it worked.

"Now, I must be going," he said. "Are
you sure you'll be all right? If you feel at all
nervous, I'm sure we could make room for you
at our house."

"We'll be fine," Harry's mother said. "Won't
we, Harry?"

Harry nodded, grinning.

"Well, then," Mr Slater said. "I know it's not
what you were hoping for, but this place is not
without value – not great value, but better than
nothing. But we can talk about that another
time. I'll pop by tomorrow to see how you are.
Good evening."

They stood at the door and waved as Mr
Slater drove away. It was very quiet when the
noise of his car died away. All they could hear

was the "shhh" of the sea on the shingle beach below the cliff, the whisper of the trees in the wind and the twitter of birds.

The light was already fading as they shut the door. They switched the lights on and closed the curtains. They weren't sure whether people in the country had to black out their windows like people in the towns.

Harry's mother warmed the pie in the oven. It was filled with chicken and vegetables and Harry thought it was the best thing he'd ever tasted. His mother laughed and they both agreed it was the best thing either of them had ever tasted – at least for a long, long time.

Harry and his mother settled down in the living room and listened to the radio and to the wind whistling round the house. Harry fetched some more wood for the fire and then his mother snoozed in the armchair while he flicked through some old magazines.

There was a sudden knock at the door and they both jumped. Harry opened the door and found a man in uniform on the doorstep – a soldier about his mother's age.

"Hello," the soldier said, and he took off his cap. "I'm sorry to disturb you. Mr Slater asked if I'd drop by. My name is Captain Morris."

"I'm very pleased to meet you," he went on as Harry's mother stepped up beside Harry. "Everything all right?"

"Yes, thank you," she said. "Won't you come in? Are you stationed near by?"

"In a manner of speaking, yes," he said. He ducked as he stepped in the door. "I'm working for the Ministry," he explained. "I'm making a record of local buildings – looking for the gems. There are soldiers down on the beach too – they're a decent bunch."

"You're rather young for a job like that, aren't you?" Harry's mother asked. Her voice was cool.

"A soft job, you mean?" Captain Morris said with a grin. "Yes, I suppose I am."

Harry's mother frowned. But then Captain Morris tapped his leg with his walking stick. It made a dull clunk.

"Lost it at Dunkirk," he said. "That's why I have a desk job. But I'll tell you, it didn't feel like a desk job yesterday when I was up on the tower of the church taking photos of gargoyles. I studied history before the war, you see. They tell me it's important work, but ..."

"I'm sure it is," Mrs Pointer said. "I'm sorry. After all – we need to remind ourselves of what we might lose."

Captain Morris nodded. "So much has already been lost," he said.

Harry looked at his mother and saw tears well in her eyes. "Yes, Captain," she said. "So much."

They looked each other for a moment and then the Captain put his cap back on.

"I'd better be going," he said. "My driver is waiting outside."

"You're staying in the village?" Harry's mother asked.

"No – I'm local. I live a few miles away. With my mother."

He smiled a shy smile.

"I'll be back tomorrow," he said. "I hope I'll see you then, Harry. Mr Slater told me about your near fall at the door."

"It was so horrible," Harry's mother said.

"Terrifying," Captain Morris said. "I've been over there and checked the lock. It seems fine, but best to stay away, Harry."

"I will," said Harry. "I promise."

"I don't want to alarm you," Captain Morris said, "but there have been a few accidents in the past, I'm afraid. Children seem to be drawn to that cliff edge. A boy at my school went over when I was about your age, Harry. Someone saw him climb over the wall."

Captain Morris shook his head before he went on.

"It must have been a shock for you both," he said. "I'm sorry it's been such a rotten time for you. You must think we're all mad here – or bad, one or the other."

"Not all, I'm sure," Harry's mother said.

"Well," said Captain Morris. "It was nice to meet you. I hope we'll meet again."

Captain Morris walked out into the dusk. Then, with one last wave, he got in the car and it drove away.

*

Daylight was fading when Captain Morris left and night fell very soon after. Dark clouds scudded across a deep blue sky.

The wind was stronger now and it made a sad moaning noise in the chimney in Harry's room when he went up to bed. He read a few pages of his book, but his eyes were too tired to focus. He switched off the lamp and settled down to sleep. He was dimly aware of something banging far off, but he was asleep in moments.

The next day, Mr Slater came back as he had promised. "This wind is getting up," he said. He was holding onto his hat. "It's going to get worse they say."

"It was rather lovely to hear the wind in the trees and the sea on the shingle last night," Harry's mother said.

"I fear it's going to become less pleasant quite soon," Mr Slater said. "We do get some wild weather here."

"It beats air-raid sirens and bombs," Harry's mother told him.

"Indeed," Mr Slater said. "We're very lucky here in comparison."

"We have to make the best of it," Harry's mother said. "We can't complain. There's always someone worse off."

"Very true," Mr Slater said. "Very true. Did Captain Morris drop by?"

"He did," Harry said. "He lost a leg at Dunkirk!"

"I remember when we heard the news," Mr Slater said. "Remember it like it was yesterday. I've known him since he was a little boy, you see. His poor mother was devastated, but look at him now. You never know what you can do until you're tested."

"Captain Morris said there had been other accidents at the cliff," Harry's mother said. "Children in particular."

Mr Slater nodded. "Yes," he said. "No need to worry yourselves, but we have storms here every now and then – bad ones. Ones that are worse than normal. In storms like those, children have been lost. What possessed them to be out here in weather like that ... Well, who can know? You know what children are like."

Harry's mother looked at her son. "I do indeed," she said, with a frown.

"There have been several deaths over the last 50 years," Mr Slater said. "There's a bad storm due now and I think that's why Captain Morris had it on his mind. Just stay away from the cliff, Harry, and you'll be safe."

"I will, sir, I promise," Harry said.

"Good lad."

Mr Slater had more food for them – eggs, bread and a jar of honey – and he refused to take any money or ration coupons. He asked them how long they were staying.

"One or two days, that's all," Harry's mother said.

Harry was delighted. He had expected her to say they would be going back that day. He let out a little cheer and Mr Slater chuckled.

Mr Slater left a file of papers for Harry's mother to look at and asked her to go to his office the next day when she'd read them.

Harry and his mother slept in – something neither of them had done for a long time – and then they had a good breakfast of fried eggs and toast. A rain shower kept them indoors and then, after a late lunch, Captain Morris knocked at the door and came in for a cup of tea.

"I wondered if you'd like me to show you the local landmarks now the weather has cheered up?" he said.

"The ones that are not under the sea?" Harry's mother said. She managed a small smile.

"Quite," Captain Morris said.

"We'd like that, wouldn't we?" said Harry's mother.

Harry agreed and they followed Captain Morris out of the house and down the road to the edge of the cliff.

"As you know," Captain Morris said, "that wall you see there is all that remains of Wickford Hall. A splendid old manor house, so they say."

He rummaged around in his bag for a moment and came to a halt.

"Here we are," he said, and he handed Harry an old postcard. "I thought you'd like to see a picture of the place."

Harry looked at the yellowy photograph. It showed a grand but rather gloomy old house. There were tall trees behind it and elegant gardens in front, with flower beds and clipped hedges, stone steps and a curved gravel drive. He passed it to his mother.

"It looks a bit joyless," she said. "We have a painting of it over our fireplace at home. It's also very gloomy."

Captain Morris laughed.

"I suppose it was gloomy," he said. "But perhaps that was how the last owner liked it. He was an odd sort."

"Oh?" Harry said. "How?"

"A rum character," Captain Morris said. "He was interested in the occult – that sort of thing."

"The occult?" Harry asked.

"Yes," said Captain Morris, and he arched an eyebrow. "Black magic and so on."

Harry's eyes widened. Captain Morris smiled.

"But his magic didn't help him in the end," he said. "Wickford Hall is under the sea, just like the rest of the village. And Lord Harrington is in it."

"He's under the sea too?" Harry gasped.

"He went over with the house," Captain Morris said. "It seems he refused to leave. The servants all got out, but he stayed."

"He sounds crazy," Harry said.

"Harry!" his mother said. "You shouldn't speak ill of the dead. And he is your great-grandfather after all."

"He does seem to have been – how shall we put it? – unusual," Captain Morris agreed. "He risked his life to save the Doom in the church when that was falling into the sea in a storm. And then he let it go over the cliff with the house!"

"The Doom?" Harry asked.

"Ah," said Captain Morris. "I should explain about that. Let's walk over to the church – or what's left of it."

They walked along the cliff edge. The cliffs were high, and they were cracking and crumbling like a huge, half-eaten loaf of bread that was shedding crumbs. Every now and then Harry could see where part of the path had fallen away.

Far below, Harry saw soldiers milling about on the beach and a line of concrete blocks and barbed wire that they had laid out along the shore to defend it from attack from the sea.

"Between you and me," Captain Morris said. "I don't think Jerry will try to land here. He'd never get up those cliffs. That's why the soldiers are over there, where there's a gap in the cliffs."

"Well, I'm glad to hear that!" Harry's mother said.

Harry looked ahead as a gull flew by on the wind. The church tower stood on the highest part of the cliff. It teetered on the edge, alone since the body of the church had collapsed onto the shingle below.

"It's only a matter of time before the tower goes over too," Captain Morris said. He pointed out to sea. "All churches are built going east to west, with the altar in the east and the tower often at the west. The Doom was in the eastern part of this place."

They arrived at the wall to the churchyard. There was a padlock on the gate.

"What is the Doom?" Harry asked.

"A Doom is a painting of the end of the world," Captain Morris said. "It shows what will happen when the world ends – the good are raised up and go to Heaven, the sinners are taken to Hell. And Doom paintings are always more interested in the Hell part. Lots of devils poking sinners with toasting forks, that kind of thing."

Harry smiled. "I'd like to have seen it," he said.

"It was a jolly fine one, and very famous," Captain Morris said.

He rummaged in his bag again and brought out another postcard. "Here it is."

Harry and his mother looked at the card. It showed a very complicated painting, with angels at the top and demons down below.

The demons stood next to a huge mouth – the mouth of Hell.

"There's a rather good story about it too," Captain Morris said.

"Oh?" said Harry, and he sat down on the churchyard wall. Captain Morris sat next to him. A seagull squawked in the tower above them.

"The story goes," Captain Morris said, "that there was one demon in the painting that had earned a rather nasty name for himself."

"How?" Harry asked.

"Well, I'm sure you know that there are some holy relics that people touch to bring them luck or to ward off evil and so forth."

Harry nodded and looked at his mother. This was what she called "mumbo-jumbo".

"Well, people here had the same idea about this demon, but in reverse," Captain Morris said. "They began to believe that this demon would do as you asked it if you wished something bad. If you wanted revenge, or to teach someone a lesson, or if you felt cheated out of something – then you would touch the demon and ask its help."

"Did it work?" Harry asked.

"Harry!" his mother said. "Of course it didn't work."

She put her hand in front of her mouth.

"I'm sorry," she said. "I'm not at all religious … I don't mean to cause offence."

Captain Morris laughed. "No offence," he said. "I'm not religious at all. But people must have believed it did work. Those were simpler times, and harder too. In any case, the Puritans painted over the Doom with

whitewash in the 1600s. We might not know
about it at all if a leaking roof hadn't washed
some of the whitewash away in the 1800s. They
say the first thing that was revealed was the
demon."

"Creepy," Harry said.

"And did people start wishing on it again?"
his mother asked.

Captain Morris nodded. "I'm afraid so,"
he said. "The vicar restored the painting, and
he was horrified. He was a very modern man,
but he decided to fight the old beliefs with
the old beliefs. And so he hammered a big
iron nail into the Doom painting, through the
demon's heart. Then he said a few prayers and
convinced the locals that the demon's powers
were at an end."

Captain Morris was silent for a moment
before he went on.

"Of course, the sea was always on the attack," he said. "The last of the village disappeared under the waves. In the end, the churchyard was locked and even the church was abandoned. People forgot about the Doom again. They should have removed it and taken it to a safe place – it was very old and important. But maybe the evil stories put people off. In the end, only Lord Harrington was willing to risk his life to save it. A terrible storm was about to take the church away, and he only had time to save the section with the demon on it, before the eastern end of the church collapsed into the waves."

"But why did he take the painting?" Harry asked.

"That we don't know," Captain Morris said. "And I don't suppose we ever will now. Perhaps that's just as well, since they say Lord Harrington was interested in dark magic himself! Do you know, my grandfather knew him – they were at school together. My grandfather didn't have a bad word to say about anyone, but he said Lord Harrington was the nearest thing to evil he'd ever known. All the village children were afraid of him."

"Why?" Harry asked.

Captain Morris shook his head. "He never did say," he said. "But I could see fear in his eyes when he talked about him. Here ..."

Captain Morris pulled a book from his bag and turned the pages until he came to the one he wanted.

"There," he said. "That's him."

Harry and his mother leaned forward. There was a photograph of a well-dressed man with a face that might have been handsome had it not had such a cruel sharpness to it. His eyes – even in this old print – glowed with a sinister kind of energy.

All three of them looked out towards
the sea, to the waves over the place where
the house and Lord Harrington lay. The sky
seemed to darken a little and the wind grew
colder.

"Come on," Captain Morris said. "I know
the chap in charge of those soldiers. He'll let us
on to the beach."

It was hard walking on the beach. It wasn't a sandy beach like the one Harry had been to in Cornwall on a holiday before the war. This was a long bank of small stones, piled up by the sea.

Harry's feet sank into the stones and it slowed the whole business of walking until he felt like a toddler again. Each crunching step sent a mini shower of pebbles tumbling down. Harry marvelled at how Captain Morris coped with only one leg. He walked nearer to the sea, where the ground was more even.

"I used to come here all the time as a boy," Captain Morris said. "I used to look for amber or pieces of flint with a hole all the way through. Look, here's one."

He stooped down, picked up a stone and handed it to Harry. It was a piece of flint, rounded by the sea and the shingle. It had a hole through the middle, not quite as big as Harry's finger.

"A little piece of gravel gets into a crack or a hole and then the sea works it around," Captain Morris explained. "It wears away and wears away until there's a perfect round hole. I used to string them together like necklaces. I still have a string of them on my door at home."

Harry put the stone in his pocket. Something caught his eye ahead in the shingle. He walked towards it.

"No further, Harry!" Captain Morris said. "We're almost under the tower and it could collapse at any time."

Harry took a few more steps to pick up a piece of rusted metal about six inches long.

"You aren't the best at following orders, are you?" Captain Morris said as he returned. "I meant it, Harry. The cliffs are very dangerous."

"Harry!" his mother snapped, grabbing his arm. "Do as Captain Morris says."

"Sorry," Harry said. He held up his find.

"What have you got there?"

Harry gave Captain Morris the piece of metal. As Captain Morris turned it over in his hand, he looked up at the church tower above them.

"It looks as if it's just come over the cliff," he said. "It's rusty, but not as rusty as it would have been if it had been in the sea. This is old, Harry. A nail, I think."

"Never mind what it is," Harry's mother said. "Don't wander off like that, Harry. I don't know what I'd do if ..."

Harry put his arms around her. "I know, Mum," he said. "I'm sorry."

They walked along the beach for a while longer and then they climbed back up the bank to the cliffs and their cottage. Harry was starving and ready for something to eat.

"Won't you join us, Captain Morris?" Harry's mother asked. "I'm sure I can rustle up enough for three ..."

"Thank you," Captain Morris said. "But I must be getting back. I said I'd be home before now."

"I'm sorry," Harry's mother said. "Of course. Your mother ..."

Captain Morris blushed.

"I think it's rather sweet," Harry's mother said. "That you live with her, I mean."

"It was hard for her when I ... With the leg and everything," Captain Morris said. "My father died a couple of years ago. It was rather sudden – the old ticker packed in."

"Oh, I'm so sorry," Harry's mother said. "I was joking – and it was in poor taste. Please forgive me."

"Nothing to forgive," Captain Morris said. "No harm done." He tapped his walking stick on the ground and looked at his feet.

"Thanks for your company today," Harry's mother said.

"Yes – thanks, Captain Morris," said Harry.

"It was my pleasure," he said. "And it's George. Call me George."

"Margaret," said Harry's mother.

"Well, goodnight, Mrs ... Margaret ... Harry. If there's anything I can do while you're here, just let me know."

Captain Morris turned and walked off into the darkness.

"I like Captain Morris," Harry said. "You do too, don't you? I know you do."

Harry saw his mother blush a little.

"He seems very nice," she said. "Now off to bed."

Harry read for a while, but when he switched off the lamp and closed his eyes, he found himself going over the walk and what the Captain had told him.

He saw the Doom painting very clearly in his mind and, in particular, the demon that had been at the centre of so many curses over the centuries.

He saw the church as it used to be before its collapse and he saw Wickford Hall too. He felt as if he was stepping back in time and seeing the area around the cottage as it was long ago.

Harry thought of Lord Harrington too – the way his eyes glowed in the darkness of that old photograph. It was such a cold, cruel face and yet, like it or not, he was related to Harry. Harry wished it wasn't true, but it was.

These uneasy thoughts filled Harry's mind as he fell asleep. The sea pulsed on the shingle beach and the wind moaned in the chimney.

What seemed like only seconds later, Harry woke with the feeling that something had touched him on the arm. He saw a shape, darker than the surrounding gloom.

"Mum?" he said.

There were more shapes now. The moon came out from behind the clouds and lit up a group of children gathered together around his bed. They were pale and their faces were filled with fear.

"Leave," they said. Their voices were quiet but insistent. "Leave."

Harry jumped out of bed, but by the time his feet hit the floor, the pale children were gone. He sat at the edge of the bed gasping.

Then he heard the banging again.

He went to the window and looked out. The moon was full and clouds were racing across the sky. Captain Morris was right – a storm was coming.

Harry now saw where the banging was coming from. The door in the cliff wall was open. It would swing open and slam back every now and then in the wind. Someone must have unlocked it. Harry wondered if it would survive the night or if it would get smashed in the wind. But even as he thought it, the door slammed shut and stayed shut this time.

First thing the next morning, Harry saw a barn owl hunting in the meadow. He threw on his clothes and sneaked out of the house to watch it.

He had never seen an owl before and was amazed to find how silent it was. It flapped its wings with as little noise as a moth as it flew over the long grass, its white face like a mask.

Harry watched the owl until it flew away in search of its prey. It was then that he noticed the door in the wall out of the corner of his eye.

He looked back at the house. He knew his mother would be furious if she saw him. But there was no sign of her, so he walked over and was astonished to find the door padlocked again.

Who had opened it and why – and when had they come back to close it? In any case, Harry was sure – 100% sure – that the padlock had been closed when he leaned on it. It was baffling.

Just then he heard Mr Slater's car heading up the road. Harry walked back to the cottage as his mother opened the door.

"Where have you been?" she called.

"There was an owl, Mum," Harry said. "A barn owl."

She smiled. "How lovely," she said. "You should have come and told me."

"If I'd moved I would have scared it off," Harry said.

Mr Slater walked over. "Good morning," he said. "I hope you've been comfortable in the cottage."

"Very, thank you," Harry's mother said. "Harry just saw a barn owl."

"Lots of those round here," Mr Slater said. "Tawny owls too. Interested in nature, are you?"

"Yes, sir," said Harry.

"Well, there are badgers in the woods at the bottom of the road. I'll have to show you them one evening, if you'd like."

"Yes please!" said Harry. "Thanks."

"We may not be here that long, Harry," his mother said. "We need to get home. We don't know anyone here."

"We do," Harry said. "We know Mr Slater and we know George ..."

"Harry, I'm not going to discuss this now," his mother said.

Mr Slater stood for a moment in the silence that followed. Harry sighed and stared back at the sea.

"I'm very sorry," Mr Slater said at last. "But could I trouble you to come with me into town? There's a file we need to look over today. It's about the house and so on. Legal papers, you know. I'm sorry."

"Oh dear," Harry's mother said. "I was hoping to spend the day with my son. Does it have to be done today?"

"I'm afraid so," Mr Slater replied. "Harry could come along. He could have a mooch about the town."

"Harry?" his mother said.

"I'd rather stay here," Harry said. "The owl might come back."

"I don't know, Harry," said his mother.

"I'll be fine, Mum," he said. "Stop fussing. I promise I'll stay away from the cliff and so on."

"It should only take a couple of hours," Mr Slater said. "Perhaps three. But no more."

"Please, Mum," said Harry. "I'm 14. Another few years and I'll be old enough to join the ar–"

"Don't you dare say that!" his mother shouted.

Harry scowled and looked at the ground. "Sorry," he said.

"Very well, Mr Slater," Harry's mother said. "Let's get going. If Harry wants to stay here by himself, then so be it."

She turned to leave and then turned back. "Don't go near that wall or that door," she said to Harry.

"I won't," he said. "I promise."

Minutes later, the two adults were driving away. Harry stood and watched them go, and he felt a pang of regret that he had not gone with them after all. He stuffed his hands into his coat pocket and found the flint with the hole in it and the rusty nail from the day before. He wished Captain Morris was there so they could explore together. The soldiers would never let Harry on the beach on his own.

Harry sat on the low wall outside the cottage and marvelled at how still it was – no sound except the faint hiss of the sea on the shingle. He hoped the barn owl might come back, but there was no sign of life on the meadow.

He walked along the track, heading for the main road, but there was nothing of interest to see, just more deserted fields. He stood for a while and watched rooks pacing back and forth in the sandy soil, like old men in black coats, digging for worms.

At the bottom of the track, Harry saw the wood in the distance – it must be the one with badgers in it. He had a half a mind to go and look for them, but he didn't in case his mother returned and found him gone.

The sky was darker now and a chilly wind was growing in strength. Harry walked back to the cottage. He was hungry and he made himself a sandwich, then listened to the radio while he ate it.

After that he rooted among the books in the living room and his bedroom, but the most interesting thing he found was an old map of the area.

He spread it out on the floor and weighed it down at each corner with books. It showed things as they were when Wickford Hall was still there. Harry could see that it was as near to the cliff edge then as their cottage was now. He was sad to realise that this cottage, too, would lie beneath the sea one day, fish flitting in and out of the oven door.

What would a deep sea diver see now if he was to walk on the ocean bed? How much of Wickford Hall was still intact? Had it all been crushed by waves and swallowed up in weed and barnacles?

As he thought about this, there was a knock at the door. Harry opened it to find a soldier standing on the doorstep. His face was in shadow.

Then the man stepped forward into the light. It was Captain Morris, and he had a rifle in his hands.

"Hello!" Harry said. "Come in. Mum isn't here."

"I know," Captain Morris said. "I've popped by to tell you there's been a spot of bother with your mother I'm afraid."

Captain Morris took off his coat and threw it over the back of a chair. He leaned the rifle next to the door.

"What's happened?" Harry asked. There was an icy sliver of fear in his heart. "Has something happened to Mum?"

"Don't be alarmed," Captain Morris said. "Mr Slater's car came off the road and your mother was hurt – it's only a bump on the head, but they want to keep her in hospital tonight just to be safe. I don't really understand it.

Mr Slater barely does more than five miles an hour."

"Can I see her?" Harry asked.

"In the morning," said Captain Morris. "There's no sense in going now. She'll be fast asleep. She asked Mr Slater to telephone and ask if I would come over. So here I am."

"There's no need," Harry said. "I'm a bit old for a babysitter, after all."

Captain Morris sat down in the armchair.

"But never too old to have a friend to visit, I hope," he said. "I'm sure you'd manage very well, but what say I kip down on the sofa tonight? Just to keep your mother happy?"

"Well ..." Harry said. "I suppose Mum would want you to. Is she really all right?"

"I'm sure she is, Harry," Captain Morris said. "If it had been more serious then Mr

Slater would have said so. You have my word on that."

Harry nodded. "Why have you got a rifle?"

"Oh," said Captain Morris. "Target practice down on the beach. I still have to keep my eye in, you know."

"I heard shots earlier," Harry said. "I wondered what they were."

"There we are then," said Captain Morris. He opened his bag and took out two packages covered in newspaper. "Anyway – the fish and chips are getting cold."

After the excellent fish and chips, Harry and Captain Morris settled down and listened to the radio. After a while, Harry showed the Captain the old map he'd been looking at and asked him if he could tell him more about Lord Harrington.

"There's not much to tell really," Captain Morris said.

"Well, what was that you said about magic?" Harry asked.

Captain Morris shook his head. "There was a craze at the end of the last century for ghosts and magic and so on," he said. "It happened again a few years back, after the Great War. So many people were killed and their loved ones hoped they might talk to them again."

"Do you believe in ghosts?" Harry asked.

"I'm not sure," said Captain Morris. "I don't think so. But then I've never seen one. How about you?"

"I don't know," said Harry. "I ..."

"What?" Captain Morris said with a smile. "Have you had a ghostly experience yourself?"

Harry squirmed in his chair. He didn't want to seem foolish, but in the end he decided to tell Captain Morris about the nightmare with the pale children and the banging door. Captain Morris listened, and he only spoke when Harry had finished.

"That must have been scary," he said. "Nightmares can seem very real."

He looked at his leg for a moment and Harry had the feeling that the Captain had nightmares himself. He already wished he hadn't said anything.

"You heard about the accidents on the cliff top with children in the past and you've dreamed about them," Captain Morris said. "It's natural to be worried."

"But I didn't dream about the door," Harry said. "Not that first time. It really was open when we arrived. I nearly fell through it."

"True," said Captain Morris. "That is a puzzler. I don't even know who has the key to that padlock. None of the chaps on the beach has a key, I'm sure of that."

"But why would anyone open it?" Harry said. His voice was louder than he had intended. "Why open it, then lock it again?" he asked. "And why did the children in my dream tell me to leave?"

Captain Morris leaned forward and put his hand on Harry's arm.

"Calm down, Harry," he said. "There are people who look at dreams and explain them. With all that's happened to you, it's no surprise you've had some bad dreams. How long has it been since your father –"

Harry jumped to his feet. "Not everything is about him!" he shouted.

Then he took a deep breath and sat back down.

"Look, sorry," he said. "I love Dad and I miss him, but if anything happens now, someone always brings up Dad. This isn't about him, I know it. There's something else."

"I don't know what to say, Harry," Captain Morris said. "I wish I had some easy way to explain it all, but I don't. Some things just stay a mystery."

Harry nodded.

"Come on," Captain Morris said. "Time to turn in. I'm shattered even if you're not."

Harry yawned even as he tried to protest, and the Captain laughed.

"Things always seem clearer in the morning," he said. "You'll see."

Harry woke to the sound of a door banging.
He looked out of the window and could see
the door in the wall opening and closing like a
mouth. The wind was wild and the house was
groaning and creaking as if the whole roof was
going to rip off at any moment.

Harry got dressed and went downstairs. He
tapped Captain Morris on the arm. He got no
response, so he shook him instead. The Captain
slept on.

"Captain Morris!" Harry called. "George!"

The Captain murmured in his sleep, but he didn't wake. Harry shook him harder this time, but still he didn't stir. The banging of the door became more insistent. Harry looked at the sleeping Captain and then towards the sound. He put on his coat and stepped outside.

The wind hurled dust into his eyes and blinded him for a moment, but he pressed on, over the meadow to the door. The wind seemed to have come around behind him like a great hand and it pushed him towards the wall – so hard it was difficult to stay upright.

It was as if the door was sucking the storm in – and Harry with it. It took all his strength to resist falling forward. He felt like he might fly through the air. The memory of being dragged through the door and out over the cliff came back to terrify him.

Within seconds, Harry was at the open door. He grabbed the wall at either side, terrified of falling through and over the cliff. But when he actually looked, he stared in amazement and disbelief.

Instead of the raging sea far below, there was grass – a lawn. There was the manor house – Wickford Hall – just as it looked in the painting at home and in Captain Morris's photograph. There were the tall chimneys, the stone steps and statues, the curved gravel drive.

It was impossible and yet there it was.

Harry had to be dreaming. That was why he couldn't wake Captain Morris. It was another dream, that was all. He stepped through the open door onto the path that ran across the wide lawn.

The moon was so bright that it sent deep shadows across the grass and the gravel, and Harry could see every detail of the Hall – every tile on the roof, every stone of the walls. The moonlight glinted on the windows and lit up the glass.

But the wind was getting stronger and the tall trees beyond the house bent and shook and roared like lions. Harry could hear the sea in the distance – the same sea that should be crashing at the cliffs below where he stood. Then the door banged shut behind him.

Harry turned at the sound. Between him and the door stood a group of children – the same grim-faced children from his last dream.

They stared at him, their eyes wide. They held out their arms and opened their mouths and tried to cry out, but their voices came out as dry whispers, like wind in dead leaves.

"Go!"

The wind grew louder and the sound of the trees and the sea roared in the air and drowned out the children's thin voices. Clouds raced across the sky and covered the moon. The garden plunged into darkness as the children moved towards Harry, and he ran as fast as he could to the house.

Harry rushed up the steps of the house. The door was open. Even as he rattled the door handle, he wondered why he had not woken up yet. This was the point in a nightmare where he would usually wake up.

Harry stepped into the entrance hall and turned to look at the window panes in the door. The moon was strong enough to show the children standing on the lawn watching the house. They were not going to follow him in.

The hall was dark, but there was a door that was a little ajar and light was coming through. Harry walked towards it.

"Hello?" he said. "Excuse me. Hello?"

There was no response and Harry carried on, opening the door and walking into a long room lit by candles. At the far end was a man with his back to Harry. He was standing in front of a painting and right away Harry knew that it was the Doom – or at least the fragment of it that Lord Harrington had saved.

"Ah, Harry," the man said. He didn't turn round. "Come in. I trust the children did not frighten you."

"Who are you?" Harry asked. "How do you know my name?"

The man turned round. It was Lord Harrington. He looked just like the sinister photograph Captain Morris had shown Harry.

But now, instead of a suit and tie, he was wearing a long black robe with a hood at the back.

"I know all about you, Harry," Lord Harrington said. "I have no choice – for the moment – but to exist in this half-life, but I can see beyond these walls. I can see you and I can see your mother. I can affect things. As your dear mother discovered this afternoon."

Harry stared at him and clenched his fists. "You?" he said. "You made the car crash?"

"No," said Lord Harrington. "I asked that favour of my lord and, since he knew it would help to bring you here, he agreed. His power grows, day by day."

"But this is a dream!" Harry shouted. "None of this is real."

"I'm afraid this is all too real," Lord Harrington said. "You are quite awake, I can assure you. Unlike that idiotic soldier friend of yours. He is fast asleep and dreaming of the happy days before the shrapnel took his leg."

"No!" Harry shouted.

"I knew his grandfather," Lord Harrington said. "A weak family. Always have been."

"Better than a mad one," Harry said.

"But you are a part of this mad family." Lord Harrington chuckled. "We are kin, you and I. Do you know my school friends called me 'Harry' as a nickname – short for Harrington, you see? We are more alike than you think."

"No!" Harry shouted.

He turned and tried to run, but the doors were now locked.

Lord Harrington ignored Harry's attempt to escape. "Your crippled friend told you about the Doom," he said. "He told you of its history and its legend. Well, it's not a myth. The Wickford Demon is all too real."

"How can that be?" said Harry, searching for some other way out. "It's just a painting."

"Just a painting?" Lord Harrington said. "I suppose it must seem like that to a boy like you. Look at it!"

As Lord Harrington said these words, he held out his hands and Harry felt pulled towards him, as if by a magnet. His shoes squeaked on the wooden floor as he tried to resist, but he was dragged along. He ended up beside Lord Harrington and the painting.

There were many demons on the wooden panel, but it was obvious which one was the Wickford Demon. The paint on its chest was worn away by the touch of so many fingers over the centuries. The wood showed through, and so it seemed to have a big black heart. And in the centre of that heart was a hole.

All the demons of the Doom were hideous and strange, but the Wickford Demon stood out even in this crowd of horror. Its eyes bulged, it had a snout like a pig's, and curved fangs jutted out of his fiery mouth – two going up, two going down. Long horns sprouted from its ugly head. He had two more faces on his chest and another where his groin should have been. His legs were scaly, grey and flaking, like a dead fish, and a spiked tail coiled around them. Long hair hung from his arms and his hands ended in huge claws like those of an eagle or a vulture, with black talons.

Whoever painted the panel all those years ago had put all his hatred into that image. It seemed to glow with evil.

"It is beautiful, is it not?" Lord Harrington said.

Harry stared at him, but it was clear he was not joking.

"Beautiful?" Harry said. "It's ..." He could not find the right word.

Lord Harrington smiled.

"Oh, it's not beautiful in the pathetic way *you* might use the word," he said. "Not beautiful like a flower or a pretty girl. No – it is beautiful in its sheer power and darkness. It is beautiful like the night or a storm."

At the word "storm", the wind answered with a bellow and the windows shook.

"You see!" Lord Harrington said. "He comes!"

"Who?" Harry asked, looking round.

"But I haven't explained, have I?" Lord Harrington said. "Forgive me. As you know,

the Wickford Doom and the demon it contained
became famous over the years. It became
known as an unholy relic – a place where
curses would be heard and, if the pilgrim was
devout, acted upon. Again and again, the
people asked the demon for favours. They
whispered curse upon curse in its ear. And
with each new curse, its power grew."

"What do you mean?" Harry said. "What
power?"

Lord Harrington waved his arm to indicate
the Hall where they stood. "This power," he
said. "We should be under the sea, but here we
are – invisible to the world and yet attached
to it. The demon did this. He will do so much
more."

Harry shook his head. "This is impossible.
It has to be."

Lord Harrington ignored him. "The vicar
knew," he said. "He was a man of science, but

still he knew the demon's power. He knew what he was doing when he rammed that nail into its heart. He would have let the Doom go over with the church, but I couldn't let that happen. I risked my life that night. I asked the demon for power. I told him I would save the Doom if he helped me and I heard a voice – a voice like none other. A voice to drive men to the brink of madness."

Harry wondered if Lord Harrington wasn't already mad.

"I made a pact with the demon that night," Lord Harrington went on. "The demon gave me eternal life and I have not aged one hour since that time."

"Eternal life?" Harry said. "What's the point of that if you live here where no one can see you? Sounds like an eternal prison to me."

Lord Harrington's eyes narrowed.

"There can be no true power without pain," he said. "These people who go to their gods with feeble prayers and sulk when their wishes do not come true ... They don't understand that gods need sacrifices. You must suffer. That is the pact."

"And this pact you made with the demon?" Harry said. "What does he get out of it?"

Lord Harrington's smile returned, wider and more wolf-like.

"Well, my boy," he said. "That is where you come in."

"Me?"

"Yes," Lord Harrington said. "You don't think I lured you here for your sparkling wit, do you? They told you about the terrible 'accidents' over the years? Those poor children who fell to their deaths in past storms? The same children whose spirits warned you to leave?"

Harry stared at him. "What?" he said. "You don't mean –"

"My master asked for seven children," Lord Harrington said. "You, my kin, are the seventh. We have been waiting for you. The same blood that flows around my body flows around yours. When you die, the contract will be sealed, the circle will be closed. The doors into the world will open and my master will walk the earth. I, too, will step back into the world, with my powers a thousand times greater. Together my master and I will rule the world."

"You're mad!" Harry said. "And we've already got a madman out there who thinks he can rule the world!"

"Pah!" Lord Harrington said. "No human will be a match for us. Without their weapons, what are they? Nothing. And their weapons will have no effect on us. Our power will make their weapons look like toys."

The wind picked up again and howled around the house.

"It is time," said Lord Harrington. He closed his eyes for a moment, and then he took a long curved dagger out from under his robes.

Lord Harrington grabbed Harry by the
throat. Harry tried to free himself, but Lord
Harrington's grip was too strong. The dagger
in his left hand glinted in front of Harry's face.
Harry tried to call out, but the grip on his
throat was too tight. In any case, who would
hear him?

Lord Harrington released Harry and shoved
him towards the Doom painting.

"On your knees!"

Harry collapsed to his knees. He could not stop himself. It was as if a ton weight was pressing down on his shoulders.

"Do you see the heart?" Lord Harrington snarled.

Harry could only groan.

"That hole there was where that stupid vicar hammered the nail," Lord Harrington said. "But I took it out. I freed my master – freed him from that iron nail, from the church and from the storm! They thought I was mad because I would not leave Wickford Hall, but I knew I would have a reward for my loyalty. They saw the cliff collapse and the Hall crash into the sea with me in it, but that was only a dream. The Hall remains, cloaked in magic. It has been here – and I have been here ever since – while the petty business of the world went on about us. There will be a new order to things when my master walks the earth."

Harry stared at the image of the demon. "Why would you want something like that to rule the world?" he asked.

"Why not?" said Lord Harrington. "Look at the fools who rule you now. Look at the chaos in your world. Look at this war you are fighting, the blood and the death."

"It's a war against evil!" Harry yelled. "You want the world to be ruled by a demon who demands children as a sacrifice."

"Are children not dying every day in your world?" Lord Harrington said. "Do your leaders not demand sacrifices? Do your people not suffer?"

"It's different," Harry said. "They're fighting a war for freedom."

Lord Harrington laughed.

"Freedom?" he cried. "To do what? To act out your silly, pointless lives? To grow ill? To know pain? To die? Does it make you feel better to know your father was free when he was shot? Did freedom make the agony less for him in the moments before he died?"

"Stop it!" Harry shouted. "Leave my father out of it! You don't know anything about him."

"Oh dear," Lord Harrington said. "I've upset you. Look. The others have come to watch. They know how special you are, you see."

Harry followed Lord Harrington's gaze and, in the glow of the candle, he saw the six pale children staring in through the window.

"They don't often come this close," Lord Harrington said. "This room has ... unpleasant memories for them."

Even in the dim light, Harry could see that the children's faces were filled with fear and sadness. He knew that their fear was for what his death might bring. It sounded crazy, but then this whole thing was crazy. If the Hall could be here after all these years, then maybe Lord Harrington was right about the demon. Maybe Harry's death would let it step into the world – and rule. Harry knew he had to do something – if not for himself, then for everyone else.

With all the will power he had left, Harry jumped to his feet and kicked Lord Harrington hard in the shin. As Lord Harrington cried out, Harry knocked the dagger from his hand and it thudded to the floor point first. It stuck up out of the floor, and the handle juddered back and forth.

Harry ran and grabbed a chair. He lifted it over his head and took a deep breath, ready to hurl it through the window in front of him. But there was no strength in his arms and, no matter how hard he tried, he could not do it.

Lord Harrington laughed.

"My dear boy," he said. "Do you think this is one of your Saturday morning movies? Do you think you can simply run away? No, no, no. Accept your fate, Harry. You have spirit, but it is wasted. There is no escape."

"Is that so?" a voice said near by.

Harry and Lord Harrington both turned at the sound. It was Captain Morris and he had a rifle aimed at Lord Harrington's head.

No one moved for what seemed like minutes.

"One move and I'll blow your head off," Captain Morris said. "Harry, come here."

Harry tried, but his legs wouldn't move. Lord Harrington smiled his wolf-like smile.

"Harry!" Captain Morris said. "Come on!"

"I can't!" Harry shouted. "He won't let me."

Captain Morris frowned as he tried to get a grip on what was happening.

"Finding it all too much for that brain of yours?" Lord Harrington said. "A Cambridge man, aren't you? I'm an Oxford man myself."

"Shut up!" Captain Morris shouted. "What have you done to Harry?"

"Nothing ... yet," Lord Harrington said. "But I do intend to kill him."

"Well, that's not going to happen," Captain Morris said. "Because if you move so much as an inch, it will be your last, believe me."

Lord Harrington smiled and stooped down to pull the dagger from the floor. Captain Morris took aim and pressed the trigger. Nothing happened.

He tried again. Nothing. Lord Harrington grinned and shook his head as if Captain Morris were a small child.

"Look at you," he said. "Pathetic."

Captain Morris lowered his rifle and stared at Lord Harrington. Then he grabbed the rifle by the barrel and lifted it above his head like a club.

"Maybe," he said. "But I'm still taking the boy."

Lord Harrington put the dagger on top of a wooden cabinet.

"Good," said Captain Morris. "Now release Harry from whatever spell you've put on him."

"Spell?" Lord Harrington said. "But you don't believe in magic, Captain. How could I have put a spell on him? How could I have restored your leg?"

"What?"

Harry could see by the Captain's face that something had changed. Captain Morris lowered his hand to his knee and stared.

"It's … It's warm," he said. "It's real. How …"

He shook his head in amazement and stamped his foot. He laughed. He jumped up and down. Tears of joy rolled down his cheek.

"It's a trick!" Harry shouted. "Don't believe him!"

"No!" Lord Harrington said. "No trick."

Captain Morris rubbed and squeezed his leg, his amazement changing to joy.

"Do you remember how you prayed that your leg might be saved?" Lord Harrington said. "Do you remember what it felt like when those prayers were not answered? You lost your faith then, didn't you? You stopped believing in anything. But you had trusted in the wrong god. My lord rewards loyalty. He will not let you down."

"My leg is as good as new," Captain Morris said. "It's a miracle!"

"The leg is truly restored," said Lord Harrington. "But there is a catch ..."

"You see!" Harry shouted. "Don't listen to him."

"As soon as you leave this place and return to your world, your new leg will be gone and the artificial limb back in its place."

"No!" Captain Morris groaned. "So it's an illusion then? I'll kill you, you sick, twisted –"

"No," Lord Harrington said. "It's not an illusion, I assure you. The leg is real. Take the dagger. Stab it. It will hurt. It will bleed. It's not a trick. Magic, yes. But not a trick."

"So this is just to torture me," Captain Morris said. He stared at the floor.

"Not at all," Lord Harrington said. "I just needed to give you something you would value more than the boy."

"What?" Captain Morris said.

"As I have explained to Harry," said Lord Harrington, "he is very special. He is the seventh child – my great-grandson. He is the last and greatest of the sacrifices. Even now my master wakes and comes to see me keep my promise to him."

"Your master?" Captain Morris said.

"The Wickford Demon!" Lord Harrington cried. "Oh do keep up, Captain. Listen. Here he comes."

The wind was roaring, but Harry could hear something else above the wind and above the sea. It was a low growl mixed with something horrible, like a thousand animals screaming in pain.

"If you allow me to complete my contract with my master," Lord Harrington said to Captain Morris, "then the path to your world will open and you will cross through. If you join us, your life will be spared and your leg restored for ever. That is a promise."

Harry looked at Captain Morris and saw him look back and forth between Harry and Lord Harrington and his leg. There were tears in his eyes as he looked at Harry again. Lord Harrington grinned.

"Good," he said, and he moved towards Harry with the dagger.

There was a loud bang, like a crack of thunder, and Harry turned to Captain Morris. His rifle was aimed at Lord Harrington, and a puff of smoke drifted across his face. Lord Harrington stared at him with a look of confusion on his face. He put his hand to his chest. It was covered in blood when he pulled it away.

"Why?" Lord Harrington said, turning to Captain Morris. "You barely know this boy. Who would ever know?"

"I would know," said Captain Morris. "Come on, Harry. Let's get out of this hellish place."

Lord Harrington laughed.

"You still don't understand, do you?" he said. "Fool! Did you think it would be so easy to defeat me? Did you think it would be so easy to end all I have worked for?"

Captain Morris cocked his rifle and aimed it at Lord Harrington's head.

"Enough!" Lord Harrington said.

He stretched out a hand and Captain Morris flew backwards and crashed into the wall a few yards behind. He sank to the floor, stunned.

"But he shot you!" Harry cried. He stared at Lord Harrington. "I saw the blood."

"Yes," said Lord Harrington. "But my life – my body – is protected here. See."

He placed his hand to his chest again and this time when he pulled it away, he held a bullet between his fingers.

"The wound is already closing," he said. "In a moment from now it will have healed. I am immune to your weapons here. You cannot win."

Harry looked at Captain Morris. He was slumped against the wall, out cold.

"The Captain cannot help you, boy," Lord Harrington said. "No one can. My master will soon be here."

Harry felt a great shudder go through the whole house as the walls shook and windows cracked. He could feel a rumbling under his feet.

"He is here!" Lord Harrington shouted in joy. "He's here!"

The storm raged and the walls began to bulge as a series of thuds shook the building. The wood panels on the walls whined and cracked and at last the wall split open and a blue light shone in.

A terrible smell entered the room and the dreadful screaming sound got louder. It was so loud that Harry put his hands over his ears, but the noise was still too much to bear. Harry closed his eyes with the pain of it, and when he opened them, he saw the demon – a horrible living mirror of the demon in the Doom painting. It entered through the smashed wall.

"So this is the boy?" the demon growled. "What is the delay? You know what you must do! Kill him!"

15

A shot rang out and all eyes turned to where
Captain Morris was getting to his feet. He
was unsteady, blood pouring from a cut above
his left eye. Harry saw him cock his rifle and
shoot the demon again. The demon snarled and
strode towards Captain Morris. His clawed feet
scratched the wooden floor and splintered it.

Captain Morris cocked his rifle and shot
again. The demon reached out and grabbed the
barrel. It looked at it for a moment before it
crushed the gun in its claws and let it drop with
a clang to the floor.

"Who is this creature?" the demon growled.

"He is no one," Lord Harrington said. "A minor problem, that is all."

The demon peered at Captain Morris. "You dare attack me?" it growled.

Captain Morris said nothing. Harry could see the terror on his face as the demon loomed over him.

"With the death of that boy," the demon growled, "the contract will be complete and I will be free to step into the world of men. For centuries they have begged me for their favours. Now I will get my reward."

"They won't give up without a fight!" Captain Morris shouted. "You forget that we are fighting evil every day out there in the war. That boy has more guts than that coward over there!"

The demon laughed. "You may be right," it said. "But that will not save him."

The demon reached forward and flexed the long curved talons on its scaly hands. "What if I take both legs from you?" it said. "How brave would you be then I wonder?" The demon clutched at Captain Morris's thigh. The Captain howled in pain as the claws dug in.

"Kill him, master!" Lord Harrington shouted.

"Be still!" the demon bellowed. It turned on Lord Harrington. "Do not dare to give me orders!"

"Forgive me, master," Lord Harrington said. He dropped to his knees and bowed his head.

The demon turned back to Captain Morris and Harry saw his chance. He pulled the nail from his pocket and pushed it into the hole in the Doom painting – the hole at the demon's heart. As soon as the point of the nail went in, the demon screamed in pain and turned to face him.

Harry pulled off one of his shoes and began to hammer at the nail with the heel. The demon clutched his chest and roared.

"No!" Lord Harrington shouted, still on his knees.

As the demon wailed and flailed about, crashing his scaly arms into the ceiling and walls, Lord Harrington seemed to suffer along with him. His face began to age, wrinkling and peeling. Harry could see the shape of his skull now and the bones under the shrivelled flesh of his hands as he reached out towards him.

"Harry!" Captain Morris shouted. "The lamp!"

Harry looked round and saw an oil lamp on a low table. He knew exactly what Captain

Morris was thinking. He picked it up and hurled it at the Doom.

The painting burst into flames, lighting up the room with a bright flash. The demon convulsed in pain and rage, and was pulled back towards the hole it had made in the wall.

Lord Harrington was almost a skeleton now, his eyes sunk back into his sockets. But even with no flesh on his face, Harry could see the hatred and fury in him. He staggered towards Harry, the dagger in his bony hands.

The demon was falling to pieces. Holes burst through its body, and blue light shone out, as it was pulled towards the hole in the wall, twitching and screaming. As it slid past Lord Harrington it grabbed him in one of its clawed hands and pulled him away with it.

The demon and Lord Harrington were dragged out the door as if a whirlwind was sucking them out through the smashed wall.

The burning Doom painting followed close behind them and – with a brilliant blue flash of light – all was dark beyond the ragged hole.

But the storm had not yet ended.

If anything its wildness had increased. The Hall was now shaking as it had when the demon first arrived. But this time, Harry guessed at another cause.

"The cliff is collapsing under us!" Harry shouted, as he ran over to Captain Morris.

"Hurry," the Captain said. "Back to the garden wall – to the door we came through. The whole house is collapsing."

He was right. It was. The end of the room gave a groan and fell away. It left behind a view of the raging sea and wild sky beyond. There was a tremendous crash and more of the house caved in and went over the edge.

They ran, with Captain Morris trying his best to keep up with Harry. The ground rocked as yet more of the cliff collapsed. Captain Morris fell.

"Run, Harry!" he yelled. "Save yourself!"

"No!" Harry shouted, and he ran back to help him up. "We're in this together!"

Harry put Captain Morris's arm round his shoulder and they stumbled across the lawn towards the door in the wall. Harry turned back and saw a huge crack in the ground snake its way towards them.

Harry and Captain Morris threw themselves towards the door as everything on the cliff side fell away. They crawled up in the darkness as the wall toppled backwards into the sea. There was nothing now except four or five feet of soil between them and the drop.

Harry staggered to his feet and led the Captain further away from the drop. There was a sudden roar and a bright light came rushing towards them. They both recoiled in terror.

A car jammed on its brakes and screeched to a halt.

"Harry!"

"Mum!" Harry yelled, running towards her.

"I was so sure something terrible was happening!" she said. "I insisted Mr Slater drive me here, poor man. The wall ..."

"It came down in the storm, Mum," Harry said. "We came outside to take a look."

"You must have been so afraid," his mother said.

Mr Slater came and stood beside them. "Come on!" he shouted above the wind. "You are all coming back to my house!"

No one argued. Harry and his mother went to the cottage and packed their bags as fast as they could. They all leaped in the car and Mr Slater set off down the road as if he expected it to crumble beneath them. He was two miles inland before he slowed down and calmed a little.

Harry's mother sat in the back with her arms around her son. Harry closed his eyes and listened to the rumble of the tyres on the road until at last there was a screech and they came to a halt.

When Harry opened his eyes he saw that they were beside a red-brick house. A woman stood in the bright doorway.

"Albert?" she said, as Mr Slater got out.

"We've got some visitors, my dear," he said. "Captain Morris. And Mrs Pointer and her son from the cottage. There's been a cliff fall and they are a bit nervous about spending the night there."

They had all got out of the car now and stood in the light of the lamp above the door.

"Come in, come in," Mrs Slater said, and she put her arm round Harry's mother.

"Perhaps a spot of brandy might be in order," Mr Slater said.

Harry and Captain Morris were left alone. They looked at each other for a minute or so, but neither was able to put what they were feeling into words. Then they followed the others inside.

The next day made the night seem like even more of a bad dream. The air was still and a thin mist pulled a veil over the far sea. Birds twittered in the hedge outside the kitchen window as Harry sat down to breakfast. Captain Morris and Harry's mother were already talking at the table.

"Cup of tea, Harry?" Mrs Slater said, as she came in from the garden. "There should be enough in the pot."

"Yes please," Harry said.

"Did you sleep all right?" Mrs Slater asked. "Not very comfortable that sofa, I know."

"I was fine, thanks," Harry said.

He caught Captain Morris's eye, trying to discover if he had told his mother what had happened.

Harry was desperate to talk to Captain Morris, but the chatter soon became quite normal – as though they had always intended to stay at Mr Slater's house. It soon sounded as if they had all been friends for years rather than hours. Harry noticed how easy his mother and Captain Morris seemed to be in each other's company. He had not seen her so relaxed since his father died.

After they had eaten, Harry offered to take the scraps out to the chickens. Captain Morris said he'd come with him, and so they managed to get some time alone.

"About what happened last night," Captain Morris said.

"I knew Lord Harrington couldn't trick you into taking his side," said Harry.

"Thanks," said Captain Morris. "I wish I'd felt so sure of that myself."

"I'm sorry," Harry said. "About your leg."

Captain Morris smiled.

"We're lucky to be alive," he said. "That's twice I've cheated death. I used to think I was unlucky, but maybe I'm the luckiest man alive. I got off that beach at Dunkirk and many good men didn't. And we got out of that hell-hole too. But we never would have if it hadn't been for you. That was quick thinking, Harry."

"But what are we going to tell Mum?" Harry asked.

Captain Morris put his hand on Harry's shoulder.

"Listen, Harry," he said. "If you want to tell her, then I'll be there to back you up. But will she ever really believe us? Will any of them? Would you believe it if you heard it from someone else? I was there and I can hardly believe it myself."

"I know," Harry said. "I've been thinking that. Mum would want to believe me and she'd want to believe you, but how could she? It's all too crazy."

Captain Morris nodded. "Then we'll keep it to ourselves?" he said.

"I don't even want that," said Harry. "I don't ever want to think about it again, never mind talk about it."

"OK," said Captain Morris. "It's a deal. Let's go back inside now. I can hear Mr Slater coming back from the cottage."

Mr Slater shook his head as he came in.

"I don't think we'd want you living there any more," he said. "The old place is still a long way from the edge, but the field is full of cracks and the soldiers on the beach say the sea has eaten away at the base still further. More will go over in the next storm, be sure of that. You know the church tower went over in the night?"

"Really?" Captain Morris said.

"So it's all gone, then?" Harry said. "Everything connected with the Doom ..."

"What a strange thing to say, Harry," his mother said.

"Harry's right, though," said Captain Morris. "The Doom has cast a long shadow over that stretch of coast. Maybe its fortunes will change now."

"Maybe so," said Mr Slater. "But I didn't have you marked down as a man who would believe in that sort of thing, George."

The Captain smiled and winked at Harry. "I seem to have started to believe overnight," he said. "Eh, Harry?"

Harry chuckled and the others looked on in puzzlement.

"Now see here," the Captain went on. "It's been very kind of Mr and Mrs Slater to put you up here, but they don't really have the room."

"Oh, we'll manage if we have to," Mrs Slater said.

"Well, that's just it," said Captain Morris. "You don't have to. My mother and I are rattling around in her house. She has plenty of room and she'd love you to come and stay."

"Well ..." Harry's mother said.

"That's settled then," said Captain Morris. "But I warn you, my mother will try and rope you into one of her committees. Evacuated children, the Women's Institute, the Parish Council – you name it, she's involved in it."

"I'd like that," Harry's mother said. "I'd like to help with something."

So that is exactly what happened. Harry and his mother went to live with Captain Morris and his mother. They all agreed that it was only temporary – soon they would go back to London.

It remained temporary for more than a year, and then it was made permanent by the marriage of Captain Morris and Harry's mother.

The war ended before Harry was old enough to be called up and he left home to study

History at university rather than to fight on the battlefields of Europe.

Captain Morris and Harry's mother turned Captain Morris's work on British buildings into a series of popular tourist guides. It seemed as if every visitor to any cathedral after the war carried one of George and Margaret Morris's illustrated guides.

Sometimes, very late at night, Harry and his new stepfather did talk about the Wickford Doom and the night of the storm. And of the demon, too, despite their agreement not to.

It was as if they wanted to remind themselves that it had been real, not just a terrible nightmare. But when they reminded themselves of the truth, they regretted bringing back those memories of Lord Harrington's wolf-like grin and the demon's terrible power.

Harry only returned to that stretch of cliff once. He was on holiday, and he cycled there on a calm summer's day and stood at the cliff edge. It looked so different in the sunshine – the church tower was gone and the wall too. The cottage was still there, empty now. Harry wondered how long it would stand as he looked down at the waves that covered the remains of Wickford Hall.

Harry had hoped that daylight, and pleasant weather, would put to rest his terrible memories of the place. For a moment or two he felt as calm as the sea below, but then he felt the old fear return.

He saw nothing, heard nothing. It was like an ice-cold, invisible hand had reached into the pit of his stomach. He turned away and walked back to his bike, stumbling in his haste, not daring to look back.

Harry cycled away, never to return.

Our books are tested
for children and young people by
children and young people.

Thanks to everyone who consulted on
a manuscript for their time and effort in
helping us to make our books better
for our readers.